Ticcing Thomas

The World's Fastest Arm Flapper

TOURETTE SYNDROME

Written by Jill Bobula and Katherine Bobula • Illustrated by Rob Hall

NORTH KAMLOOPS
AUG 1 3 2009   1018441740
E BOB
Bobula, Jill, 1965-
Ticcing Thomas, the world's
fastest arm flapper, Touret

Wildberry
Productions

www.wildberryproductions.ca

Brought to you by Wildberry Productions
as part of the WE ARE POWERFUL® children's book series.

WE ARE POWERFUL®

Thompson-Nicola Regional District
Library System
300-465 VICTORIA STREET
KAMLOOPS, BC   V2C 2A9

No part of this publication may be reproduced in whole or in part, or stored in a retrieval system, or transmitted in any form or by any means, electronic, mechanical, photocopying, recording, or otherwise, without written permission from the publisher, Wildberry Productions. For information regarding permission, email bobula@wildberryproductions.ca.

ISBN 978-0-9784095-2-4

Text copyright © 2009 by Wildberry Productions.
Illustration copyright © 2009 by Wildberry Productions.
WE ARE POWERFUL ® 2009 by Wildberry Productions.
Desktop publishing by Janine Frenken.
Photography by George Karam.
Edited by John Hall.

www.wildberryproductions.ca

All rights reserved.
Published by Wildberry Productions.

Wildberry Productions would like to recognize the Lowe-Martin Group for their generous support of the WE ARE POWERFUL® children's book series and their contribution toward children's mental and neurological health issues.

Printed by The Lowe-Martin Group
Printed in Canada

First Wildberry Productions printing, April 2009.

Disclaimer: This book contains general information about children's neurological disorder. Readers should consult health professionals for appropriate medical advice.

Library and Archives Canada Cataloguing in Publication

Bobula, Jill, 1965-
    Ticcing Thomas, the world's fastest arm flapper, Tourette
Syndrome / Jill Bobula and Katherine Bobula ; illustrator, Rob Hall.

(We are powerful children's book series)
ISBN 978-0-9784095-2-4

    1. Tourette syndrome--Juvenile fiction. I. Bobula, Katherine, 1960-
II. Hall, Rob, 1965- III. Title. IV. Series: Bobula, Jill, 1965- . We are
powerful children's book series.

PS8603.O28T28 2008   jC813'.6   C2008-907309-6

1018441740

This book is dedicated to all those touched by Tourette Syndrome.

We believe individuals with Tourette Syndrome hold a special place in our world.

"Ticcing Thomas is an exceptional opportunity for teachers to raise the consciousness levels of their students, for parents to help shape their children into more tolerant and informed grownups, and for kids to discover new kinds of diversity and uniqueness in their peers. Thomas tells his story with a humour and directness guaranteed to bring comfort to youngsters who have TS and satisfy the inquisitive minds of those who don't. There are valuable life lessons in here, tender issues skillfully addressed and differences embraced. I can only wonder at the kind of world we'd live in if school libraries had a whole section devoted to books like the ones in this series. Bravo!"

    Rosie Wartecker
    Executive Director, Tourette Syndrome Foundation of Canada

"Tourette's Syndrome is a disorder of brain that affects thinking and behaviour. There is considerable burden associated with this condition imposed on those affected and their families. Repetitive involuntary movements, actions, and/or vocalizations can be frustrating to children with Tourette's. Equally or even more wearisome is the stigma associated with the disorder and the increased risk of victimization and discrimination stemming from prejudice and ignorance.

In this book Jill Bobula and Katherine Bobula allow information about the condition to become accessible to younger readers in a simple and yet inclusive narrative. This knowledge can be an important ingredient to exalt the self esteem of affected children, and also far reaching as a vehicle to dismiss the stigma fed by apprehension and misunderstanding."

    Abel Ickowicz MD, FRCPC
    Psychiatrist-in-Chief, The Hospital for Sick Children, Toronto, Canada

"All children deserve the safety and comfort of well informed peers. Thomas, like any other little boy or girl wants to belong. This book will prove useful on the journey."

    Honourable Linda Reid, B.Ed, M.A., M.L.A., Minister of State for Child Care, Province of British Columbia

My name is Thomas and I'm the world's fastest arm flapper. I like to jump up and down and flap my arms. Some people call me Ticcing Thomas, others say I have Tourette Syndrome, also called TS. I love who I am because I'm such a great kid! My Tourette Syndrome is a very precious gift.

My mom and dad tell me I've had Tourette's since I was born. When I was a baby, I would sit at the table and flap my arms as if I was about to fly away. There are many things that are special about me. Keep reading and find out what makes me so awesome.

Mom says I always had more energy than other children. And dad tells me I was so fast no one could keep up with me. Even my father can't flap his arms as fast as I can, but it's funny to watch him try.

It's not easy having Tourette's, especially at school. Sometimes when I'm in class, I want to jump up and down and flap my arms. This is one of my tics.

I have tics because there's a lot of energy inside of me. I feel this energy mostly when I'm excited, nervous or tired. The energy just keeps building and building – like the lava inside a volcano just before it erupts.

It's a lot of work to keep all this energy inside my body! But I've learned a few tricks.

For instance, when I need to stay focused, I try to get rid of all the extra energy before too much builds up. Sometimes, I just want to get up and run as fast as I can – which is really, really fast – flap my arms and blurt out sounds. If I put a yellow card on my desk, my teacher, Ms. Lee, knows I need to release my extra energy. It's our little secret code.

Ms. Lee sends me to a special place to release my extra energy before recess. I do my tics and then I'm ready to play outside with my friends.

Ms. Lee is great because she knows I'm not doing something bad or trying to get attention. She understands how I feel and how hard it is for me to always feel safe around others when I do my tics.

I also have a verbal tic. Sometimes I say things out loud. I feel like a balloon letting out the air. Words come out of my mouth but they're jumbled together. "Blaout hya ayoo." They even sound funny to me.

I have a facial tic. This is when the muscles in my face make all kinds of grimaces. My friend Josh loves the way my face can change so quickly. He's really a great friend.

Tourette Syndrome is more than just having a tic. I also have trouble sleeping at night.

I can become anxious too. This means I become really nervous when there are big changes in my life. When I moved to a new school, I was really nervous and scared.

I know most kids would feel the same way too. I ticced all the time, during class, after class, at home, even when I took a shower. I was pretty tired by the end of the day.

It takes more time for me to adjust to new things in my life than most kids. Ms. Lee gives me a schedule with my activities and their times for the day. This way I can get ready for them.

Eating healthy foods is important for someone who has a lot of energy, especially for someone like me. Good food helps me feel better.

People with Tourette Syndrome can have different tics. Not everyone with Tourette's is sad and anxious or has sleeping problems. We're all different and special.

My friend Shane has Tourette's and his tic is coughing.
His coughing is not the same as a sick cough.

Now and then it sounds like Shane is clearing his throat. He makes really loud noises and sometimes it sounds like a moose call.

When someone stares at me or makes fun of me, I just tell them I have Tourette's. They usually smile back at me slightly embarrassed. I don't want people to feel uncomfortable so I explain how Tourette's works. It changes how they treat me.

Last week I was so excited in class, I was jumping up and down.
One of my classmates, Jane, told me to stop jumping. I told her I had
Tourette's but I don't think she understood.

I told my mother what happened at school with Jane. Together, my mom and I agreed that a presentation on Tourette Syndrome will help my classmates better understand what I have and why I do my tics.

Ms. Lee thinks a presentation on Tourette Syndrome is a great idea. Tomorrow is my big day.

THOMPSON-NICOLA REGIONAL DISTRICT LIBRARY SYSTEM

I'm both a bit nervous and excited about my presentation.
I know it's important to talk about Tourette's to my classmates.

Here it goes...

I'm glad I did my presentation. Everyone was listening carefully to what I was saying. My classmates had lots of questions such as "Can you catch it like a cold?" or "Does someone grow out of it?" "Is it only boys who have Tourette's?" and "Where does it come from?"

I even gave examples of different people who have Tourette Syndrome including a hockey player, a soccer player and a composer. One of the first dictionaries was written by Samuel Johnson, who also had Tourette Syndrome.

I'm really proud of myself today. I did a great job explaining what Tourette's is to my friends. Now I know they won't laugh at me.

Some of my classmates even told me about some of their problems too. Dakota told us how difficult it is for her to stay focused during class and Eddy explained how he has a hard time sitting still in his seat all day.

At first, I didn't want everyone looking at me and thinking I was different. But now I know everyone likes me for who I am, no matter what I do. I have very cool friends.

Now I know it's okay to be different. My tics are part of me and I love who I am. It doesn't really matter that I have Tourette's. I may look funny when I'm jumping up and down and flapping my arms, but I'm proud of who I am. My Tourette's is a gift. I think I'm a very special person.

The "WE ARE POWERFUL®" children's book series was conceived and designed to introduce the lives of eight children affected with various disorders, syndromes and learning disabilities. Each book brings to light the experiences of these children affected with Attention Deficit Hyperactivity Disorder, Attention Deficit Disorder, Asperger's Syndrome, Tourette Syndrome, Fetal Alcohol Spectrum Disorder, Obsessive Compulsive Disorder, Dyslexia and Dyspraxia.

The books familiarize the reader with the daily joys and challenges these children experience in their home and school setting. Children affected by these disorders, syndromes and learning disabilities are gifted in many ways. The "WE ARE POWERFUL®" children's book series was written to help children, parents, educators, health practitioners, and the public in general develop a greater understanding of each condition.

Katherine Bobula is a registered nurse with a Bachelor in the Science of Nursing and a Masters in Education. She is an international speaker and consultant specializing in children's mental and neurological conditions including learning disabilities. Katherine has a special interest in Asperger's Syndrome and Fetal Alcohol Spectrum Disorder. She is also a certified presenter for the Tourette Syndrome Foundation of Canada.

Jill Bobula is a graduate of psychology from McGill University. She is a speaker for the Tourette Syndrome Foundation of Canada and is an advocate for children's mental and neurological health issues. Jill's son has Tourette Syndrome.

Katherine, Jill and Rob